# Half title

Hey friends,

Please forgive me for having spelling and grammatical mistakes in my texts. At least in the German books, laugh. I grew up speaking and writing English since my childhood. German spelling and grammar was never my forte. I never wrote any books before 2021/2022 either. Thank you and happy reading.

Your, B. E. Wasner.

B. E. WASNER

RÉSUMÉ- OR THE STORY OF MY LIFE/

IT'S JUST PLAYING THEATER!!

IT'S TWO BOOKS IN ONE JUST AGAIN!

BOOK ONE- AUTOBIOGRAPHY

BOOK TWO ARE ROLE PLAY STORIES!

ONCE AGAIN WRITTEN AND TRANSLATED FROM GERMAN BY B. E. WASNER.

AUTOBIOGRAPHY

# Imprint

Bibliographic information from the German National Library: The German National Library lists this publication in the German National Bibliography; detailed bibliographic data can be accessed on the Internet at http://dnb.dnb.de .

Produced and published by: BoD – Books on Demand, Norderstedt

ISBN: 978-3-7568-8552-7

Special thanks to my wonderful girlfriend in the United States for proofreading this book for me. I love you sis. ♥ ☺ ☼

And thanks to my wonderful bookstore ladies, for telling me where to go to with my stories to get them printed. With the help of which I could get many great books over the years!

**ABOUT 1975**

# BOOK ONE

## CHAPTER ONE

Hi my name is Berta Edith Schulz, I was born on March 30th. 1953 at 8:10 am in Frankfurt/Main, West Germany, as the daughter of a nurse and a US Army soldier. When I was about six months old, I went to the USA with my parents. From 1953-1956 we lived in Connecticut, USA. My father was around this time in the Korean War. In 1956 we moved to the Panama Canal where I contracted meningitis in 1958 at the age of about 5 1/2. The disease is almost like polio, only much worse because this disease attacks the brain cells deep in the head and destroys them forever. At the time I became ill, almost nothing was known about it other than that there were different variants and that it was almost always fatal. We were 5 children that got sick at the same time. The only one who survived is me, despite of being blind for 7 weeks, despite of having a tracheotomy using a breathing tube to get air, despite of the fact that I was totally paralyzed from the neck down. I was taken to the death room and my mother was told that the child would not live much longer. In spite of all the medication I've been given. I saw the light at the end of the tunnel and was almost there; could feel the warmth, then I was pulled back into life at the age of 6. But not as the healthy child I once was that could even read and write. No, I came back as a newborn that can't even hold its head up or has a solid spine, but like a baby that first has to learn everything it needs to live. Because the love of a mother was stronger than death. God took me back, gave birth to me a second time. In 1959 he went to San Francisco, California, USA. A doctor once said to my mother when I was only 6 years old, "The child will never walk alive, it would be better if she were dead." I proved the doctor wrong. A little later, my father said to me, "If you don't start using your right hand as well as your left hand, I'll get the ax and chop it off, then you don't need it anymore. Then you can get a hand prosthesis. So I learned how to use that hand. In 1960 I started school and for the first two years I had lessons and physiotherapy together on the timetable. In 1962 I was in the 3rd grade and didn't want to go to school any more, my stupid teacher wanted us all to be able to write perfectly in cursive, and I was glad that because of my disability I was just able to use block letters. Then I would be transferred back to the second grade. The best thing that could happen to me. In 1960 my grandmother died in California. On New Year's Eve 1962 we flew to Frankfurt/Main. We lived in Giessen until 1966. Where I went to the American Elementry School from 1963 3rd grade, to the end of the 4 th grade. Then I went to Miller Hill in the 5th and 6th grade until April 1966.

3 years, from Sept. 1966 to Jun 1969 I was in the 7th to 9th grade of Junior High School. Then 1969, I was in the 10th grade Senior High School for a month.

In April 1968, 3 weeks after my 15th birthday, my mother passed away. In 1969 we finally went back to Germany. In April 1970 my father and stepmother got married.

1970-1971 I went to the Peter Peterson Primary and Secondary School in the 8th class of the Secondary school. I was 17 years old at that time and had no interest in boys. Instead, I talked to my teacher about the differences be-tween the school systems in the USA and Ger-many. I heard from my father that I was a slut, a whore, a bitch and that I was a lesbian. But on the other hand, he said, "If you come home with a kid in my belly, I'll kill you!" That's no joke, nor is it a joke with the ax and my hand as a kid. A while later I was first in the American Psychiatric Hospital in Frankfurt /Main, then in the State Psychiatric Hospital in Giessen, where after a few months my father accused me of having tried to kill my family in my childhood with rat poison. Then he blamed me for my mother's death, saying if I had died back then at the age of 6, my mother would still be alive! That was in the 1970's.

1974-1975 I lived in Isny, Allgaeu, where I had done my vocational training as an office worker. On St. Nicholas Day, December 6th, 1974, I got engaged to Mr. G. Wasner. Two years later, on June 30, 1976, the wedding took place. We were together for 7 years until we got divorced in 1981. My name is Wasner, my maiden name is Schulz. For a while I was in the WfB= workshop for the disabled in Herbsteln, then where I lived now, and here since 1996 in the day care center, and back in 2009 for a few years in the workshop for the disabled.

Hospitalizations: 1958- because of my illness with total paralysis and tracheotomy. 1959- Army Hospital, San Francisco, USA. 1973 I got a hip, groin and equinus surgery in Giessen, 1976 appendix surgery, 1985 hysterectomy. In the 1980's and 1990's I had 2 bladder surgeries. In 2003 bladder operation no. 3. And the last operation was for a stoma in 2019. I got my driver's license in 1985 and I drove my cars for about 25 years. I've been at home for years now and have been bound to a wheelchair for about 1 ½ years. I can't stand anymore, I can't walk anymore either.

In 2009 I started writing a little story for an online role-play game playing in the future with friends in the Star Trek world. And then in 2016 another he part of the story into the year 2378, with me having parents coming from two planets in outer space with special talents. Born on one home planet and raised on both home planets, living later on earth by my guardian and teacher, Uncle Bouthsberry. A third part of the story was added in 2021/2022, it's a fantasy novel printed in the first version in German with 106 pages. In July 2022 there where a few changes and additions made. The Story that a friend is proofreading now has in German 158 pages. And "Résumé-or the Story of my Life", is book no. four. I hope to get the books out and printed between October and November 2022. I hope to get the proofread book in German out by this time too.

# CHAPTER TWO

# TABULARY

Résumé of my life contents :

First name : <u>Berta</u>

Middle name : Edith

Surname : Schulz

Nickname : Bunny

Born: March 30, 1953

Place of birth: Frankfurt am Main, Germany.

Mother: was a nurse .

Father: was a US Army soldier.

Places where I have lived:

1953: Six months long in Frankfurt am Main,

Germany

October 1953-1956: in Connecticut, USA.

1956-1959: in Panama, Middle America, near the Panama Channel Zone.

1958: in Panama getting sick with an illness that is almost like polio only much worse. Paralyzed from neck down to my toes and blind seven weeks long.

1959: in San Francisco, California, USA after recovering a little bit.

1959-1960: we moved farther north near Santa Rosa, California, USA until 1962.

1962: New Year's Eve we moved to Giessen, West Germany, until April 1966.

1966-1969: we lived near Santa Rosa again until October.

1969: in October finally moved back to West

Germany for good. We lived in Frankfurt am Main again until 1971. Then my parents build a house farther north where I lived until 1974.

1974-1975: I was in Isny, Allgaeu where I did vocation training as an office worker.

1974: I got engaged to Mr G Wasner, on December 06 St Nicholas Day. That is the day when the holy St. Nickolas comes and brings children gifts.

1981: I got divorced from Mr. Wasner but I kept my surname "Wasner".

1985: I made my driver's license.

The End.

**BOOK TWO**

**IT'S JUST PLAYING THEATER!!**

**3 THEATER PLAYS= ONE OF THEM IS MERRY & THE OTHER TWO ARE DRAMA !**

**3 ACTS PLAYED AT DIFFERENT TIME IN DIFFERENT PLACES!**

B.E. Wasner

**ROLE PLAY**

# ACT 1.

## SO EBBES! / NOW SO WHAT?

R&K: Excuse me, is there still a seat here?

W: Yes, sit down! Do not we know each other?

R: No, I don't think so. We live at the Maison del Rent, but we both go here for coffee on Fridays.

W: I'm in a daycare.

R: Oh, there's a civil servant there, isn't there?

W: Yes. R: We have one too, but our Zivi is terrible! K: Oh god, oh god, so awful!

W: Why terrible?

R: He's so unpunctual! He's late every morning!

W: Oh, our civil servant always comes on time, but then he falls asleep in the day care center!

K: Ebbes! – Now so what.

R: Then ours is always on the go somewhere, it's never there when you need it.

W: Our Zivi is always there, only he is constantly playing cards or something else.

K: Ebbes!  - Now so what.

R: Our civil servant always chews gum, like that......

W: Our civil service always licks ice cream, so......

K: Yuck! ugh!

R: Our civil service is messy too, so messy!

K: Oh god, oh god!

W: You can't say that about our Zivi, he is very local, only his old sneakers are always flying around somewhere.

K: Ebbes! - Now so what.

R: He's always wearing a cap, even when he's eating, always!

W: Ours had sooo..... Long ponytails, and now he has them cut!

K: Ebbes! - Now so what.

R: You have to tell him everything twice!

W: You don't need that with ours, you have to write everything down twice!

K: Ebbes! - Now so what.

R: And forgetful, he forgets everything!

W: Our civil service never forgets anything. well; only me sometimes at the Sparkasse, I wait for hours.... for days.... for weeks.!

BREAK

W: I will never forget our Zivi!!!

R&K: We would have liked to have had a civil servant like that!

THE END

# Act 2. /PLAY ONE

Christmas Party Performance 199.....

## THE DEATH OF THE MONARCHY- PART I:

## THE END OF AN UNHAPPY LOVE!

Princesses with maid:

Princess: Make me beautiful, my lover (Prince Ali) is coming soon. How much longer can I keep it a secret from the queen?

Maid: Not long now, she says; and pulls the princess's hair. OWAH!!

Prince Ali enters: My beloved princess, today I will ask your mother, the queen, for your hand!

Princess: I've been waiting for this for a long time, my prince. Queen & Prince K. enter:

Queen: This will be your future husband.

Prince K.: The wedding is next week!

Princess: No, I don't want him! I love another!

Prince Ali: I want you, even if I have to die for it.

Prince K.: Then let the weapons decide. I challenge you to a duel.

Queen: Send for the second.

Second enters the stage: Choose your weapons! (He puts them back to back and counts to 5). They aim at each other. Prince K. shoots Prince Ali. And Prince Ali, Shoots the queen dead with his last breath.

The princess yells: You killed my loved one! And grabs her gun. She shoots Prince K.

The maid waits and steals the princess's gun and says, "That's for taking so long to wait on you!" She elopes with the second!

**THE END**

## Act 3. /PLAY TWO

## DEATH OF THE MONARCHY PART II: THE END OF ANOTHER UNHAPPY LOVE!

ACTORS:

KING TUNGSTEN

QUEEN MARIE-KRISTIN

PRINCESS AYLYA

MAID BEATRICÉ

PRINCE IRONHEARTED

 KNIGHT KUNIBERT

SQUIRE ROBIN

"Behold my queen, my king, three horsemen are approaching our castle! Do you know who the horsemen are, my king?" "Yeh, it's Prince Ironhearted & Knight Kunibert with his squire Robin. Let the festivities begin!" Prince Ironhearted to Knight Kunibert, "I'm curious about the princess, we've been promised since childhood to each other!" In reality, he is thinking, 'Oh my god, if only it were all over.' "Is your bride beautiful?" Ask Knight Kunibert, the pre-occupied prince. "You know that's not easy to say. Judge for yourself!" Meanwhile: Princess Aylya sadly sits in her chamber, and don't quite know what to do. She is startled when the large wooden door opens and is relieved that it is only her maid. She immediately notices that something is wrong! "What is it that saddens you so, my child?" she asks in awe. "IT'S ONLY MY

HEART THAT ACHES SO MUCH!" Admits the princess in absent. 'I can understand very well how you feel. But you must realize that there is nothing you can do about marrying Prince Ironhearted.' 'I know Beatrice, but why can't my parents see that I don't love this prince! He doesn't love me either!' the princess complains to the maid, with whom she can talk about anything. "But you must also consider that this marriage is very important for the peace in the neighboring kingdoms. You are promised to the prince and if the promise is broken, a war will not be in sight!" Tried to explain the maid. "I love Robin." The frustrated princess said. "And nobody can do anything about that! But he's just a simple squire. In the eyes of the law, he's not worthy of you!" The maid seethes inwardly because she is also in love with the handsome squire and Princess Aylya does not allow herself to be happy with her beloved. So, a few days later, she decides to tell the Royal Parents that her good daughter is having an affair with the squire Robin. "You lie!" The royal couple is outwardly furious. "The prince and princess are promised to each other. From birth." The king summons the knight Kunibert. Without further ado, the king bribes the knight Kunibert to get his squire out of the way. "Look, it has come to my attention that the princess and your squire are having an affair!" "Ah, ha!" emphasizes the knight. "You opened my eyes my king, how can I thank you?" "Kill your squire! You will receive a piece of land as a reward." He gets involved be-cause he gets a piece of land that he has been looking for a long time! That same night he goes to his squires. "I have to kill you guys Robin." "Why sir?" asks Robin. "You have committed a great debt, you have an affair with the princess, confess!" "You are right sir!" "Then you must die! By order of King Wolfram." That same night he killed the squire, and two days later the princess was married to the unsympathetic prince. But during the ceremony, the maid rushed to the al-tar and stabbed the groom to death in order to avenge the squire's death. Everything ends in chaos. "Why this bloody deed?" Everyone asks, at a loss. "Why the bridegroom? He has nothing to do with it?" asks the king. The maid has put the dagger aside. Nobody sees that the princess takes the dagger. She leaves the chapel, distraught, and disappears into her room. There, a few minutes later, she stabs herself in the heart with the dagger. Because she can't bear the thought of being responsible for the deaths of two people.

**THE END**